JUDGED

A Forbidden Love, You Choose Your Steam Factor series, Book 5

Daphne Dennis

NOTE: These books contain two endings to suit YOUR preferences.

Do you prefer a romance with just a little steam? Read straight through, but STOP when you get to the **!

Do you prefer it hot and steamy? Skip the — chapter and go straight to the ** at the end.

Both chapters will have the same name, so choose if you're milder -- or ready for the heat **!

Judged by Daphne Dennis

Published by TLM Publishing House

2200 Belcourt Pkwy, Roswell GA.

https://www.ttpublishinghouse.com

Social Stamina – 1,2,3 Let's Go!

Titles to help look at things from other perspectives and strengthen your mindset.

The Great Ascension–1,2,3 Let's Go!

Titles to help you gain focus and climb the ladder of success!

How to Start – 1,2,3 Let's Go!

Titles to help you with step-by-step, must-have knowledge of the business world and personal experiences.

Top 10 Questions to Ask Before You…1,2,3 Let's Go!

Titles with must-have questions (and logic behind) for many of life's daily and major decisions.

Find our fiction below!

https://www.ttpublishinghouse.com/legendsreborn

https://www.ttpublishinghouse.com/7wishes

https://www.ttpublishinghouse.com/mallcadet

Social Media

Facebook: tlmpublishinghouse

Website: www.TTpublishinghouse.com

Want to Read for Free?

You may qualify for a spot on our Advance Reader Copy group.

Never heard of an ARC Group?

Simply put, it's a small group of people who are interested in a specific genre and are invited to read books before they're published.

Your feedback can help alter the storyline or even catch an elusive typo!

You're asked to provide an honest review when it is published, and that's it!

You read for free!

Go now to confirm your interest in the ARC Group!
https://www.ttpublishinghouse.com/joinTLMarc

Contents

*Note: ***indicates steamy/erotica****

The Win

"To Darren!"

Darren chuckled and took a sip of his wine, bowing his head as his co-workers patted him on the back and toasted him. He wouldn't deny that he enjoyed being the center of attention now and then, but they truly all had reason to celebrate themselves as well.

"Please, guys, this was a team effort," he said, raising his hand. "This case wouldn't have been such a success without each and every one of you. You put in the work and we crushed it in court. You should all be proud of and celebrate yourselves, okay? Now, let's have a great time."

He had made it a policy at the firm a few years ago to always have a small celebration after they won a big law case. It boosted the morale of his staff and let them know that he appreciated their work.

"You're too humble, Dad."

Darren turned to find his eldest son, Corey approaching him. Corey was the spitting image of his father. They had the same strong, square jaw, both towered over most people with their over 6-foot frames, and shared the same soft and expressive deep brown eyes. Corey had gotten his mother's complexion; a soft caramel that was a few shades lighter than Darren's own skin. Darren had been so proud when Corey had decided to become a lawyer like him. He loved his other two children, Marcus and Nia unconditionally but he and Corey had always had that special bond.

"I don't know what you're talking about, man," Darren rolled his eyes at his son. Corey was his right-hand man at the law firm and the only person who saw every step of work that Darren did. Because of this, Corey was also probably the person that knew him best in the world.

"I'm talking about all the late nights you spent in here and all the favors you had to pull to get us this case," Corey said pointedly. They had just won a big case against one of the biggest corporations in the city for their clients, a small non-profit organization that has accused the organization of plagiarizing their products and trying to bully them into silence.

Darren and his firm had spent the last five months on the case with multiple of his lawyers working on it directly and others helping with trial preparations and research. Still, it had been Darren who had taken the extra step of making contact with dozens of the corporation's employees before finally finding one who agreed to blow the whistle. It was that final testimony that had brought them the win, but most of the people in the firm just assumed that the employee decided to blow the whistle on his own.

"None of that matters," Darren waved him off, "and it doesn't diminish all the hard work that everyone did, including you." Corey had been the head attorney on the case and Darren had watched with pride as his son fought passionately throughout the case.

“Yeah, you’re right,” Corey nodded. He leaned back against a desk beside his father. “I’m just worried about you, Dad.”

“Worried? Why?”

“I know you were using work to distract yourself from everything with mom this past few months,” Corey said without beating around the bush. “The case is over now and you don’t have anything to hide behind anymore. I just don’t want to see you crash.”

Darren shook his head and took another sip of his wine. He had known that Corey would eventually bring up him and Sheila’s separation, but he hadn’t expected it to be brought up so soon.

He sighed deeply. “What do you want me to say, son?” he asked.

“I don’t know, anything? Just tell me how you feel.”

“I don’t know what I feel! She said there was no passion anymore and she was right. We haven’t had a real conversation in maybe years.” Darren sighed again. “I don’t blame her for leaving. She wasn’t happy. She wasn’t unhappy either, but I think she deserved more than that.”

“Dad-”

Whatever Corey was going to say was cut off by the doors to the firm swinging open. Both men turned to the entrance to see who had come in so loudly.

A woman stood in front of the open doors. She was wearing a black skirt suit with a white blouse and was scanning the room like she was looking for someone.

“Who is that?” Corey asked.

“Let’s find out.”

Darren approached the woman. As he got closer, he was able to properly take in her features. She had a round face with soft and delicate features except for her sharp green eyes. Her hair was pitch black and fell down her shoulders in soft waves. She had a small mole above her lip that stood out due to the bright red lipstick she was wearing.

"Good evening, ma'am," he greeted as he got closer to her. "Are you looking for someone?"

"My name is Amelia Montgomery," she said, sounding slightly hesitant. "I'm looking for Darren Cross. I want to file a lawsuit."

"I'm Darren Cross," he said, holding out a hand for her to shake. "Miss Montgomery, we're closed for the day already," he informed her. So, if you would come in tomorrow, we can discuss whatever you need to."

"This can't wait," she said firmly.

"It's going to have to."

"I want to file a lawsuit against Governor Adams."

Darren's eyes widened at her words.

"What's going on, Dad?" Corey approached them and put a hand on Darren's shoulder.

"I'm going to talk to Miss Montgomery in my office," he informed Corey. "Don't let anyone disturb us."

"What's this about?" Corey asked, confused.

"No one comes in my office, okay?" he repeated as he led the woman to his office.

He shut the door behind them and gestured to the seat across his desk. She took a seat as he did. She wrung her fingers as she sat, stone-faced otherwise.

"Okay," he said, once they were both settled. "What's this all about?"

"Governor Adams," she repeated.

"Yes, you mentioned him. And what exactly is it that you want to sue him for?"

She took a breath, steeling herself before she replied, "Sexual harassment."

Darren's eyes widened again.

"And do you have any proof of this?" he asked.

"I'm the proof," she spat out. "Me and God knows how many other women."

"What's your relationship with the governor? How do I know you're not just trying to slander his name?"

"I work at the governor's office as an administrative assistant," she replied. "And I've been there for about five years now, most of Governor Adam's term. I started as an intern two years into his first term and I've been there since."

"And the sexual harassment?" Darren asked hesitantly.

"Governor Adams has always been a very... handsy man," she said uncomfortably. "Back when I was an intern he would touch my arm or elbow or whatever and I didn't think much of it. He was always talking to me, asking me how I was and whether I was enjoying the job. I liked the attention, you know? He was the governor. Then, one day," she trailed off, paused for a second. Darren didn't know whether to prompt her to continue or not but she shook herself slightly and proceeded.

“One day, I was at the water dispenser, bent over to fill my bottle and I felt someone grab me.” Her voice was cool and detached, her eyes fixed on a spot over Darren’s shoulder. “It was the governor. I jumped and asked why he was standing so close and he said he just wanted to say hello. It became more common then. He would hold onto my waist, or grab my ass. Stand too close to me. I didn’t say anything because what could I say? He never did anything too overt, but he only stopped after I started going out of my way to avoid him.”

“You say you’ve been working there for five years and this happened when you were an intern,” Darren said. “That’s five years ago. Why are you bringing it up now? Why not sue years ago?”

"Because I was scared, dammit," she snapped, fixing her gaze on him. Her green eyes blazed with fury. "I was scared, and I honestly still am. But the bastard needs to be stopped. We get so many interns every year and I've watched him do this for years. The girls we have this year are so young. They don't deserve this. No one deserves this."

She was panting slightly by the time she was done and Darren examined her closely. He didn't think she was lying. She was too passionate to be making things up. But, did he want to cross the governor's office? His firm had tackled many high-profile cases, but those had always been in the private sector. Taking on the governor was a whole different tier.

"Miss Montgomery," he started.

"Amelia."

"Amelia. Look, I understand that all of this is... horrible. And I'm so sorry that you went through that. But, honestly, I don't know if I can represent you." He watched her face crumble but steeled himself to carry on. "This case is just a bit too high profile for us. The risks involved in suing the governor and losing... I can't put my firm through that."

Her look of devastation morphed to one of anger and disgust.

"Do you know why I came to you?" she asked. "Because I heard that your firm was the best in the city. Not just because you win your cases, but because you help the little guy. I heard that you and your firm actually cared about doing the right thing. I guess that was wrong."

She pushed back her chair and got to her feet. Darren rose as well.

"It's not as black and white as that," he argued. "Filing a case against someone in the public eye is one thing, but a governor is something else entirely. If we lose the case or get dismissed before trial, both you and my firm would be ruined."

"He is guilty," she said firmly. "And it's supposed to be your job to prove that. You think I don't know this is risky?" she scoffed. "I'm willing to take the risk to do the right thing. And if you won't pick up this case, I doubt anyone else will," she said. "But I will help the girls in that office, even if you won't. If I have to leak a story to the press or catch him in the act, I swear he won't get away with this any longer."

She turned around and stormed out of his office.

Darren watched the woman as she walked out. Her rage was evident in every step that she took and he understood it. She had been right. He didn't only pick cases for the money or the glory. He defended people that needed it the most, and he prided himself in that. Would he be able to sleep that night knowing that he had rejected Amelia? Knowing now what was going on in the governor's office. He would never be able to pretend like he didn't know now. And he couldn't let Amelia do something as stupid as talking to the press.

With a resigned sigh, he rushed out of his office after her. She couldn't have gone too far, and as he entered the main hall he saw her talking to Corey. The rest of his staff were still drinking and socializing, unaware of the potential catastrophe he was about to bring them into.

“Amelia!” he called. Both she and Corey looked over.

“She says you refused to represent her?” Corey asked. “What’s the case?”

“We’ll discuss it tomorrow,” Darren said, stopping in front of the two of them.

“Tomorrow?” Amelia asked.

“Yes, tomorrow, in our first official meeting,” he said. “We’re going to be having a lot more meetings if we’re going to come up with a solid case against Governor Adams.”

Corey’s jaw dropped in disbelief as Amelia’s lips spread in a stunning smile.

The Visit

Darren was starting to understand just how stubborn Amelia was. They had already had two meetings so far, and she had spent the entire time pushing for him to file the lawsuit immediately. He had explained time and time again that things didn't work that way, but the woman was persistent.

He was standing in his bedroom that morning, adjusting his tie as he got ready to head to work when he heard footsteps approaching. He didn't think much of it as he had both a maid and a cook, but then the door to the bedroom opened and he looked up, startled.

His wife, Sheila, stood at the doorway. She was lovely at her age, her features held only the faintest of wrinkles and her hair was always impeccably styled. She was always so put together. She had been, even when she told him five months ago that she was moving out.

“Sheila.” He wasn’t able to hide his surprise. “What are you doing here?”

She had moved out the same day she mentioned it to him, so he could only assume that she had planned it for a while. She had moved most of her belongings in the months since then but a few clothes and other items remained at the house.

“I thought you would have left by now,” she admitted. “There’s a necklace I’m looking for that may still be here.”

He gestured to their once shared walk-in closet. “Please, feel free.”

She walked in stiffly, brushing past him as she headed for the closet.

"Congratulations," she called out, her soft voice filtering out from the room. One of the things he had noticed immediately after she left was the quiet of the house. It wasn't because her absence took away the sound, but rather, her absence highlighted to him that there hadn't been sound in the house for a while. Neither of them was a fan of TV, preferring to watch things on their own devices, and the nature of both their jobs meant that they couldn't share too many details of their work- he as a lawyer and her as a therapist.

Still, it had been jarring to realize that the bone-deep silence he faced in her absence had been present for years, and he just hadn't noticed. He had realized that the two of them barely even spoke. Hearing her voice now was like a clear bell ringing through a deserted land. Why hadn't they talked more? When had they stopped talking at all?

“On what?” he asked belatedly.

“The non-profit case you just won?” she replied. “It was all over the news. I wasn’t sure if it would be awkward to text or call but I did follow through and Corey told me how hard you worked on it. Well done.”

“You don’t have to feel any type of way about reaching out to me, Shcila,” Darren said. “I that we’re not great right now, but I’m still your Darren.”

Sheila came out of the closet, holding on to a jewelry box. “You haven’t been my Darren for years,” she said with a melancholy smile. “We haven’t been anything to each other but glorified roommates for a while.”

“Is there another man?” he asked, knowing that he was coming off desperate but not caring. “Is that it?”

“Would you really care if there was?” she asked. “We haven’t had an emotional conversation in ages and it’s been even longer since we had sex. So, would it matter to you if I slept with another man?”

Darren didn't respond, but he knew that his silence was answer enough. Maybe he would go through the motions of outrage if Sheila cheated on him, but she was right, he had lost that claim on her years ago.

“There was another man,” she admitted. “We ended things just before I moved out.”

“If you ended things then why are you still moving out?”

“Because this isn’t about him,” she said. “It’s about me. I need to find what makes me happy, and the one thing I know is that this marriage isn't it. It's not even about you either, Darren. You were a good husband. Are a good husband. We just both got caught up."

She walked towards the door and pulled it open. Before she left, she gave him one last look over her shoulder. "Don't let yourself get caught up in your head about this, okay? This is good for you too. Find what makes you happy outside of work."

She left him with those lingering words and Darren headed to work with a heavy heart.

***

Darren Cross was starting to really annoy Amelia. The man didn't understand the urgency at all. She had thought that once she told a lawyer her story she would have gone through the hardest part of everything, but she was wrong. The waiting was the hardest part.

It had now been two weeks since Darren had agreed to take on the case, but they hadn't made any substantial moves since then. In the two meetings they had, he had only asked her questions with painstaking detail and had her describe her experiences with the governor.

Meanwhile, she had to come back to the office every day and watch the man continue to make every woman in the office extremely uncomfortable. On top of that, she was riddled with anxiety daily that he would find out about the lawsuit before they got a chance to file.

"If you act differently or say anything before we file the lawsuit, you'll give him time to get his affairs in order. We don't want that. He could pay off people to stay quiet or hide evidence. So, just act normal, okay?"

That was what Darren had said to her, but Amelia was finding it increasingly more difficult to do just that.

The office cubicles were not so high that she couldn't see what was going on at other people's workstations, and that was exactly what she was doing now. She was specifically watching one of their new interns, a young girl named Bella. She was incredibly hardworking and determined. Amelia liked her a lot.

Bella was just done with high school and was interning at the governor's office before heading off to college to study political science. She was one of the brightest teenagers Amelia had ever met, always asking questions and eager to do whatever work she was given at the office.

She was also very beautiful, which was turning out to be a liability. Amelia could see all the same signs that she had experienced when she was just an intern. Governor Adams called Bella to his office often. He stopped by her cubicle frequently and started casual conversations with her. He even gave her rides home after work on some days. The girl seemed to be enjoying the attention at first, but Amelia was starting to note that it wasn't the case any longer.

Bella was standing at her workstation, and the governor was leaning against the cubicle wall to talk to her. The angle that he stood at blocked anyone's view of his and Bella's bodies, and there were only a few people that shared this workspace anyway. It was lunchtime so the office was mostly empty- Amelia had only stayed behind to wrap up a proposal she was drafting. The governor hadn't seemed to notice her.

"I don't think that's really an appropriate conversation topic," Bella was saying to the governor as Amelia strained to listen.

"Come on, Bella, I just want to get to know you better," the governor replied. "You don't have to answer anyway, I already know the fellas are lining up to get with a pretty young thing like you." He chuckled lightly and Amelia couldn't see what he was doing from where she was, but Bella took a step back. "Even the old ones like me should be lining up for a taste, shouldn't we?"

"Governor Adams," Bella started.

"Governor Adams, I think you're making Bella uncomfortable," Amelia spoke up, rising to her feet. Both the governor and Bella turned around in surprise at her voice with the governor taking a few steps back.

“Amelia, I didn’t see you there,” he said, straightening his tie.

“Yeah, I’m sure you didn’t,” she replied, glaring daggers at him.

“Bella and I were just chatting,” he explained.

“Well, Bella and I have lunch plans, so if you would excuse us.”

The governor glanced between the two of them before stepping back. Bella ducked her head as she walked past the governor and Amelia put her arms around her.

“Are you okay, Bella?” she asked the girl once they were out of hearing range. “Did anything happen?”

“I’m fine,” she replied shortly, tucking her short blonde hair behind her ears. “Nothing happened, please don’t make a big deal out of this Amelia.”

“You know you can talk to me about it, right,” she asked gently.

“There’s nothing to talk about!” the girl replied, snatching her arm out of Amelia’s and storming off.

Later that day, Amelia sat across from Darren Cross and narrated the encounter to her.

“There’s more there than she’s saying,” Amelia said. “I just know there is.”

“If she’s not willing to talk, there’s nothing we can do,” Darren said.

“Do you always drop matters so easily?” she asked.

"I don't go after dead ends. If the girl wants to talk she will eventually. For now, you have to focus on people that are willing to speak up at the trial. Do you have any idea of other women at your office who have worked at your office previously that may be victims of the governor?"

“I’m not sure,” Amelia mused. “I have my suspicions, especially from past interns we’ve had, but I’d have to ask around.”

“You can’t be too loud or obvious about it, okay?” Darren reminded her. “Find out what you can quietly. We’ll find out the rest after we’ve filed the suit.”

Amelia left his office feeling worse off than when she had arrived. She was about to call a taxi home when she realized that she had forgotten her briefcase at the office. That meant she would have to head back there before heading home. Resigned, she hailed a cab and told the driver her office address.

Working hours were officially over but Amelia knew that there were always some stranglers that stayed back to work well into the night. That meant she didn’t have to worry about the office being locked. She paid the cab driver and stepped out, just as two figures were walking out of the office.

Holding back a gasp, she realized that it was Governor Adams and Bella. The girl looked uncomfortable as the governor led her into his car. She watched as Bella said some things to the governor and made as if to walk in the opposite direction but he pulled her back and ushered her into the car.

Things may have been even worse than she thought, Amelia realized. She had to get this case off the ground as soon as possible.

She headed into the office quickly after that to grab her things and head home, but she couldn't stop thinking about Bella. She hoped desperately that the young girl was okay. Amelia remembered what it felt like to be young and ambitious and have the governor taking an interest in her. The man was in his late forties but he still had a charming smile and personality that had earned him the admiration of most people.

She had tried to pretend that none of it happened for years, or tried to soothe herself with words like 'he didn't do anything too bad' or 'at least he didn't go all the way' but those words were empty. He had disrespected her and touched her inappropriately and he would continue doing the same to many more girls if she didn't do something about it.

Second Thoughts

"What if I'm making a mistake?"

Amelia voiced her concerns to the only person she knew she could talk to about them. Stella and she had been best friends since college, even though Amelia had been a public administration major while Stella had gone for music production. The two couldn't have been any more different but somehow they had made it work all these years.

When Amelia had just been a fresh college graduate and gotten her internship at the governor's office at the young age of twenty-four, it had been Stella she went to first to celebrate. Amelia's father had died a few years after she was born and her relationship with her mother wasn't the best. During those hard years of college, Stella's family had become her own with Stella becoming the sister she never had.

Now she lay on Stella's couch while her friend sat on the floor in front of the coffee table tinkering with her work. Every now and then she would play a small snippet of music out loud and ask for Amelia's opinion but they both knew that Amelia didn't know anything about music.

"I don't think you are," Stella answered Amelia's question. "What you're doing is very brave, in fact. I don't know if I'd be able to do the same."

"I'm not even doing anything yet since Darren Cross still hasn't filed the stupid lawsuit!"

Stella chuckled at her friend's impatience. "Were you able to get any of the women at the office to talk?"

"Some people said that they'd noticed the governor being pervy to some of the interns and Darren says that's enough to make the case but we're going to need an actual victim to testify if we want to bring it home," Amelia explained.

"So, you have to reach out to some past interns?"

"Darren says he'll handle it once the lawsuit has been filed."

"You've been spending a lot of time with Darren Cross," Stella said, wagging her eyebrows mischievously.

"Don't give me that face, it's not like that!" Amelia exclaimed, tossing a throw pillow at her friend.

"Are you sure? Because I've seen the man and, honey, if you're not going to hit that, I am."

"He's like fifty years old!"

"And? You're about to be thirty and he's damn fine for fifty. Trust me, you could do worse."

"Okay, I'll admit that he is incredibly handsome," Amelia said reluctantly and Stella let out a whoop of joy.

"I knew it!"

"But that doesn't mean anything!" Amelia was quick to add. "There's nothing like that between us, okay?"

"If you say so," Stella shrugged with a cheeky grin. "But I've got my eyes on you."

Amelia rolled her eyes at her friend's antics and lay back down on the couch.

*

"Okay, so what have you got?" Darren asked Amelia.

It was a few days later, and, according to Darren, they were getting very close to building a solid case.

Amelia pulled out some documents from her briefcase.

"I asked around the office if anyone had noticed the governor acting icky towards any of the interns or any women and I got some answers. Some people wondered why I was asking but I just mentioned that I'd seen him lurking around Bella so I wanted to know if it had happened before."

She pushed forward a list of names. “These are the people who I believe would be willing to give statements.” She showed him another list. “These are the names of past interns that at least two of my co-workers mentioned that they had noticed the governor took interest in.”

Darren picked up both lists and examined them. "This is great work, Amelia," he said, putting them down to smile at her. "If you decide to leave the governor's office, you'd do great as a legal aid here."

Amelia shook her head and laughed. “I admire what you all do, but politics is my passion.”

He gave her a studious look that morphed into a smile. “I can see that,” he nodded. “Well, with this I think we have enough to build a case. Once discovery starts, I’ll begin to reach out to your co-workers for statements and to these ladies to see if any of them would be willing to be witnesses.”

“So, we’re finally filing?” she asked hopefully.

“We’re finally filing,” he confirmed.

“Don’t get too excited,” he laughed as she jumped to her feet in excitement, pumping her fists in the air. “Once we file, we declare war. They’re going to deny the claims, and they’re likely going to come after you. The governor’s lawyers will probably offer you money to drop the case.”

"I would never," Amelia said vehemently. She wasn't doing this for money or fame. She was doing this because she knew what it felt like to hold the guilt and shame of a man's actions, and she didn't want any other girls to have to go through that.

“That’s good,” Darren nodded. “Just remember throughout everything that they can’t touch you, okay?”

“Do you think they would try anything bad?” she asked nervously.

“They may try to intimidate you, but they can’t hurt you, Amelia, okay?”

His deep brown eyes bore into hers and Amelia realized that she trusted his words.

"Okay," she said softly.

She couldn't tear her gaze away from his and he didn't look away either. This left them staring into each other's eyes. A knock on his office door jolted them out of it.

Amelia looked away as Darren's son, Corey, entered the office. He looked between the two of them with an undecipherable look before heading to his father to show him something.

What was that? Amelia wondered to herself.

*

"So, you and Amelia," Corey said slyly.

Darren choked on a bite of food he was eating and took a sip of water to push it down. He and Corey were having dinner the next day after filing the lawsuit. Darren had been right about the storm that this lawsuit would bring their way.

Immediately after he had filed, the governor's lawyers were down his throat to revoke the case or have Amelia settle outside of court. Since he had no intention of doing either of those, they had to go into the discovery stage of litigation. That means that he would have to work with the governor's lawyers and start getting ready to prepare whatever documents they ask for.

He could already imagine the amount of stress this entire process was going to be, but it was worth it for the ecstatic tone of Amelia's voice when she had called to let him know that her former co-workers said that the governor and his lawyers were scrambling around the office all day. She had already put in her two weeks' notice and worked her last days at the office. Though she had been sad to have to quit, Darren had reminded her that she couldn't sue the governor while still working at his office.

"There's nothing between Amelia and me," Darren replied to Corey.

“That’s bull,” his son said. “I’ve seen the way you two look at each other. What are you scared of?”

“I’m not even divorced yet, son,” Darren said.

“You’re the one who said it had been over between you and mom for a while now,” Corey pointed out.

“That doesn’t mean I’m ready to, what, date again. I’m over fifty years old, for God’s sake.”

“That doesn’t mean you can’t date or be happy, dad,” Corey pointed out. “Whether you want that with Amelia or not is up to you, but I really think there’s something there.”

“And I really think we should be focusing on the case for now,” Darren countered.

Corey sighed but backed down. “Do you really think we have a chance of winning this?”

Darren thought on it for a second but he knew his answer. "I wouldn't have taken it if I didn't think we could win. Our key would be getting those past interns to talk. I'm going to start making the calls tomorrow. I need you to start on depositions."

“Of course,” Corey nodded.

“I’ll send you the names of people you need statements from.”

The two discussed a few more matters about the case before Darren remembered to bring something up that he had been meaning to for a while.

“What about you, son?” he asked.

“What about me?” Corey echoed, confused.

"You're trying to get me to make a move on Amelia," Darren explained, "but what about you? When are you finally going to ask Christy to marry you?"

He was talking about Christina, his son’s girlfriend of three years now. Christina was practically a member of the family already and he and Sheila had often wondered why Corey didn’t pop the question yet.

Corey rubbed his neck awkwardly as his father continued to stare him down.

"Honestly did, I don't know," he admitted. "I just feel like I'm not ready yet."

"You love her, don't you?" he asked.

"Of course, I do."

"Then you're ready," he said simply. "You two are in love. And you're perfect for each other. Don't let your anxieties lead you to lose her."

Corey exhaled and nodded. "You're right. I'll work on it."

"Good man."

They passed the rest of the dinner with less heavy topics and both went their separate when they were done.

Darren still found it weird to go back to his home and not find Sheila there, even after all these months. The house was never empty thanks to their staff, but he felt lonelier than ever. He went into the bedroom and stripped methodically, taking off his shoes and socks then shirt and pants. He had just taken off his glasses and lay back on his bed when his phone started to vibrate.

He answered the call, surprised at who was calling.

"Amelia?"

"I'm sorry for calling so late," she said, voice slightly shaking.

"Are you okay?" he asked. He couldn't place the emotions he was getting from her voice.

"I'm fine, I'm just," she paused for a moment. "Governor Adams called me," she said.

"What did he want?"

"What else? He wants me to drop the lawsuit."

"Did he say anything?"

"He called me some things," she said quietly. "Said I was never any fun and that's why he stopped paying attention to me all those years ago. He practically admitted to harassing me and he didn't even care!"

“Did you record the call or anything?”

“It was a private number,” she said. “I was too shocked to think of that. He said his lawyers are going to bury us.”

"He's wrong," Darren said, trying to ensure that his conviction carried over through the phone. "We have a solid case and we are not going to be intimidated, okay? He can't hurt you anymore, Amelia, and soon he won't be able to hurt anyone else thanks to you. Remember that."

“Okay,” she said, taking a few deep breaths. “You’re right. You’re right.” She paused again before murmuring, “I’m sorry for bothering you with this so late.”

“It’s no bother at all,” he assured her. “You can call me any time, okay?”

“Okay,” she replied. “Thank you, Darren. For everything. Goodnight.”

“Goodnight, Amelia.”

He hung up and lay back down on his bed.

Could Corey have been right about the two of them? Even if Corey was right, Darren didn't know if he was ready to date again. He hadn't been single for almost thirty years. He didn't know how to be a boyfriend or lover or whatever Amelia would need. No, he could only be her lawyer and, maybe when all of this was over, her friend.

War Begins

Depositions were difficult. That was the one thing that Amelia had discovered since they filed the case. Since she had quit her job at the office, she had had much more free time on her hands. That meant that she was spending a lot of time with Darren and Corey as they worked through the case.

She didn't realize how much work went into building a case until then. According to Darren, they were still months away from a trial which meant months of waiting and doing nothing. Amelia had enough money saved that she didn't feel worried about things like bills, but she hated the thought of being idle for so long.

At least, she still had things to keep her occupied for the time being. She and Darren had been working on acquiring and compiling different records and pieces of information they would need for when the case went to trial. There had been a lot of back and forth between Darren and the governor's lawyers, but Amelia had been pleasantly surprised to find out that Darren was the kind of man that dug his feet in the dirt when faced with opposition.

The governor's lawyers had requested to depose Amelia which Darren had explained meant that they just wanted her to give a record of her allegations to them. She had been extremely nervous about that, but Darren had assured her that he would be with her the entire time and she could refuse any questions they asked her.

Their questioning had been ruthless and cold-blooded. They asked the same things that Darren did- why hadn't she tried to sue years ago when the harassment allegedly took place? But they asked it cruelly, implying that she was making up the entire case and trying to slander the governor. When she tried to defend herself and started to get annoyed, Darren calmed her down with a warm hand on her elbow and informed the governor's lawyers that his client wouldn't be answering any more questions along that line.

Darren had also been requesting a deposition with the governor but to no avail. He had sent a statement saying that he denied all the allegations but it wasn't enough for Darren or Amelia. They both knew that there was no way he would agree to sit and let Darren question him but his refusal to sit for questioning spoke volumes more than if he had agreed.

The governor's lawyers had also requested all documents about Amelia's time working at the governor's office. That had led to a long night of her and Darren sitting in her living room with papers strewn all around them as he helped her select the relevant documents.

That was when he had told her about Sheila. It still hurt her to think about how lonely the man probably was.

"So, I noticed that you have some pale skin where a wedding ring should be," she had noted idly while he scanned through some documents.

He had looked down at his hand, almost as if he's forgotten.

"My wife and I," he's started hesitantly, "we're ending things. It's been a few months now, but it's still weird, you know?"

It had only taken some gentle prodding for him to explain how he and Sheila had drifted apart over the years. She sympathized with him, even though she had never gone through such an experience. The longest relationship she had ever had only lasted about a year and she hadn't bothered much with dating since.

Still, she could understand being lonely.

Since that day, it felt like she and Darren formed a bond that went deeper than just a lawyer and their client. Amelia had managed to get three of her co-workers to give statements and she and Darren had spent time interviewing each of them to get as much information as they could.

The first interview with the receptionist, Dottie, went very well. Dottie had observed many situations where the governor would offer to give some of the interns a trip home and insist even when the girls refused. She had also seen the senator get handsy with many of the interns either as they were walking by or stepping out of the elevator.

Dottie had been nervous to give her statement at first, but Darren had quickly assured her that she wouldn't have to testify in court and that they just needed her statement to build the case. Amelia had then questioned her gently and shared some of her own experiences with the governor which had prompted Dottie to speak freely.

After talking with Dottie, Darren turned to Amelia with a smile.

"That went really well," he said, grinning.

"Only because you reassured her so much about her legal rights as a witness," Amelia said.

"Are you kidding? She only got comfortable enough to share after you connected with her like that," Darren replied.

"I guess we're just a winning combo," she said cheekily.

"The dream team."

They had used that method of Darren's strong and sound legal counsel and Amelia's gentle understanding with the other two witnesses and gotten strong testimonies from them that didn't leave the governor looking too good. Darren had handled the depositions of the governor's witnesses with Corey, but he had called Amelia every night to let her know how they went.

"What we really need," Darren was telling her as they sat in his office one evening eating take out from boxes, "is a witness for the trial. We get their statement now and convince them to testify in court. That will bring the whole case home."

"Well, you have the list of interns I gave you," she pointed out.

"I know," Darren said, "and I'll start working on them tomorrow, but I'm not sure if it'll be enough. We need that girl, Bella."

"Bella wouldn't want to testify," Amelia shook her head.

"We have to try."

Amelia wasn't so sure, but she reached out to one of her friends in the office to get Bella's phone number.

She called the girl and put the call on speaker between her and Darren.

"Hello?"

"Hey, Bella, this is Amelia."

The girl's voice went steely. "I don't want to talk to you."

"Hold on, Bella!" she cried before Bella could hang up. "Look, I know you said before that you don't want to talk about it, but you've seen the news, right? You're not the only person who may have been hurt by the governor. I want to help you."

"There's nothing for you to help with," Bella gritted out.

“Hey, Bella, my name is Darren Cross, I’m Amelia’s attorney,” Darren spoke up.

“You have a lawyer there? Is this some kind of trap?” Bella exclaimed.

"No, Bella, it's no trap!" Darren said quickly. "We just want to talk to you and ask you some questions. Look, I know all of this sounds really scary, and you're worried about so many things. You don't know how it's going to look if you speak up or whether you're going to be able to pick up the pieces afterward. But, I promise, Amelia and I just want to help you. You shouldn't keep this to yourself. Let us help."

The teenager was silent on the line for several long minutes and Darren and Amelia glanced at each other, unsure of where this was going.

“Like I said,” Bella said finally, voice devoid of emotion, “there’s nothing to talk about.”

She hung up harshly and the two slumped into their seats.

“Well, that went just about how I expected it to,” Amelia said.

"That's okay," Darren sighed. "We can still make it work with one of the past interns. I'm going to start making calls tomorrow."

Amelia nodded and got to her feet. She packed up the trash from their dinner and tossed it in the can. "I better start heading home," she said.

"Do you want me to give you a ride?"

"No, don't worry. I know you want to sink into that chair and keep working," she teased.

"You know me so well," he replied fondly, and Amelia realized with a jolt that she did. She knew that Darren cared deeply about his cases and that there was no way that he was okay with Bella not testifying. He probably wasn't pushing it because he didn't want to make Bella, or Amelia, uncomfortable.

Pulling out her phone she sent a quick text and a few minutes later, she had an address which she gave to a taxi driver.

Bella's parents lived in a townhouse that wasn't too far from the office. She knocked on the door hesitantly, knowing that Bella wouldn't be happy to see her. A nice-looking older woman answered the door.

"Hello, how may I help you?" she asked.

"Good evening, ma'am, my name is Amelia. I'm looking for Bella, I work at the governor's office with her," Amelia explained.

"Come on in," the woman gestured her in.

"Thank you, ma'am."

"Please, just call me Mary. Bella's up in her room, I'll go get her."

Amelia looked around the house as Mary went up to call Bella. There were framed pictures of Bella as a kid everywhere, as well as pictures of Bella with Mary. She noted that there wasn't a man in any of the pictures.

"What are you doing here?"

Amelia turned at the venomous tone of Bella's voice.

“I wanted to talk in person,” she said. “Is Mary your mom? She’s a very sweet woman.”

“Yes, she is my mom, and I hope you didn’t mention any of this to her,” Bella warned.

“I didn’t,” Amelia assured her. “But you should. Whatever the governor has said or done to you, he shouldn’t get away with it.”

“I’m not having this conversation with you,” Bella said turning around.

“Fine, then I’ll do the talking.”

Bella paused and Amelia took it as her opportunity to start talking.

"I've been working at his office for nearly six years now, you know? I started as an intern just like you. And I also felt so special when he started paying more attention to me. I thought it meant I was doing my job right. He'd call me into his office to talk about things or ask my opinion. It's the same for you, isn't it?" She didn't wait for Bella to respond, just kept going on.

"When he started getting touchier I brushed it off at first. And I kept brushing it off until he would full-on grab my ass in his office and I would somehow convince myself that it didn't mean anything. He eventually stopped when I started avoiding him, but he never truly stopped. Do you know why I'm speaking up now after all these years? It's because of you, Bella. I see you in the office and how passionate and determined you are. He doesn't get to take advantage of that. And you shouldn't let him."

Amelia finished her speech and waited patiently for Bella to say something. The girl remained with her back turned and Amelia was sure that she was going to get rejected again when Bella's shoulders started to shake. Amelia rushed to her and put her arms around her and Bella turned into the embrace, sobbing on Amelia's shoulder.

Amelia shushed her and patted her back soothingly as the young girl cried in her arms. She had been right- it was much deeper with Bella than she had known. When Bella eventually calmed down, she pulled back from Amelia's arms.

"I'll tell you everything," she said in a small and broken voice.

"Okay, sweetie," Amelia said, wiping away her tears. "You don't have to talk now, okay? Just come to me when you're ready." She gave her Darren's card as Mary stepped into the room, worry etched on her face at the sight of her daughter crying.

Amelia left their home feeling both outraged at the governor and elated that they had gotten Bella to agree. She didn't think before giving the cab driver Darren's office address.

"Darren!" she called out as she came in. She knew that he would be the only one left at work by this time.

"Amelia?" he asked, standing as she came into his office. "What are you doing back here?"

"I talked to Bella," she said breathlessly. "She's going to testify."

“What?”

“Bella is going to testify!” she said. “We have the bastard!”

Darren let out a sound of joy and rounded his desk, wrapping Amelia in a hug and spinning her around.

“How did you get her to talk? In fact, don’t answer that, you’re amazing!”

“I just talked to her,” Amelia giggled at Darren’s enthusiasm as he put her back on her feet.

They were standing only inches apart, breathing hard with face-splitting grins on their faces.

“You’re amazing,” he repeated, staring into her eyes.

She didn’t know what to say, didn’t know who moved first, but suddenly they were kissing. Darren held her firmly by the wait with his other hand coming up to cup her face. Amelia sighed into the kiss and deepened it, parting her lips to let Darren’s tongue into her mouth.

They kissed passionately for some moments before Darren suddenly pulled back.

“What is it?” she asked as he took a few steps back from her.

“We can’t- we can’t do this,” he said.

“What do you mean?”

“This!” he gestured between them. “It’s not a good idea.”

“I think we’re a bit too late for that,” she said. “There’s clearly something between us, we can’t just pretend like there isn’t.”

“I’m not pretending. All there is between us is friendship and a professional relationship.”

“That’s not true, Darren.” She took a step closer and reached out but he dodged her hand.

“I think you should go,” he said, looking away from her.

Amelia stared at him in disbelief before picking up her bag and storming out of his office, slamming the door behind her.

--Showdown--

Amelia was a fool.

She had been an idiot to think that she stood a chance with Darren, but became a certified fool when she had walked out of his office that night and lingered at the door, waiting for him to come after her. He never had and now, two months later, they had lost that easy connection that had built so beautifully between them.

Bella had eventually reached out to her, and both she and Darren had been present as the young girl shared her story. The governor had done more than just touch her inappropriately at the office but had assaulted her countless times, forcing kisses and unwanted touches on her whenever he gave her a trip home after work.

He kept her silent with the threat of ruining her name if she spoke up, but Darren assured her that he wouldn't let that happen. After they had heard Bella's testimony, Amelia wanted nothing more than to talk to Darren, share her feelings and fears and listen to his thoughts on the matter. Instead, they had shared a charged look but ultimately gone their separate ways.

And that was why Amelia considered herself a fool. Because after everything she still believed that he wanted her, that he had feelings. She didn't know why he was denying them and she wasn't fully convinced that she wasn't being completely delusional.

Nevertheless, they continued to work together until the trail day eventually approached.

"Are you nervous?" she asked him as they sat in the courtroom waiting for the judge to arrive.

“I should be asking you that,” he responded.

“I'm never nervous when you're with me.” Her reply was more honest than she wanted it to be, but it was the truth. Darren made her feel brave.

Her words seemed to shock him but before he could respond, the judge arrived and the trial began.

It was a harsh back and forth between the two sides, but Amelia was proud to see Darren hold his ground the whole time. He made a passionate opening statement, citing Amelia's years of work and the governor's charming façade. As the trial went on, the opposition brought forth witnesses to attest to the governor's good name, and Amelia herself had to testify.

But, it was Bella's testimony that brought the case home. The whole court was silent as the young girl recounted her experience with the governor. Bella wasn't the crying girl Amelia had held in her home on the stand. Instead, she was the strong-willed and determined young woman Amelia had witnessed countless times in the office. She didn't allow her voice to waver as she talked about the way the governor forced kisses on her and grabbed her in his car then dropped her off at her home with a threat to remain silent.

With Bella's testimony over and the jury gone off to deliberate, Amelia knew that the case was theirs.

"We have a celebratory party," Darren informed her. "After every big case, we win. It's on Friday at the office if you want to come."

They were standing outside the courthouse after the judge had declared the governor guilty, and while Amelia felt pride and satisfaction in their hard work, the feeling was bittersweet. With the case over, she truly had to say goodbye to Darren and she wasn't sure if she was ready for that.

"I'll think about it," she said with a shrug, knowing that she probably wouldn't show up. It was better to end things now than to drag it out.

"Okay," he said.

She waited still, foolishly, hoping he would say something but he just walked away.

*

Darren knew something was wrong when he didn't even want to celebrate. It was another win for the firm and a personal win for him, but he felt dejected as he stood amidst his partying staff.

"You okay, dad?" Corey asked.

"Yes, son, I'm fine."

"You sure?" he pressed. "You don't look like someone who just won a sexual assault case against a governor."

Darren gave a small laugh at his son's words.

"I guess I'm just tired."

Corey hummed noncommittally. "Is Amelia going to come?"

That was the question, wasn't it?

"I don't know," Darren replied honestly.

"Hey, baby." Corey's girlfriend, Christine wrapped her arm around him from behind and placed a kiss on his cheek.

“Hey, Darren, congratulations again on the win,” she said.

“Thank you, Christy.”

“Did Corey share the big news yet?” she asked.

"Big news?" Darren looked at his son confused.

“Oh, babe, I don’t know if this is the right time,” he trailed off as Darren’s gaze landed on the ring on Christine’s finger.

“You did it!” he exclaimed, pulling the two of them in for a hug. “I’m so happy for you both!”

“Thanks, dad,” Corey said bashfully.

"It took him long enough!" Christine playfully slapped her fiancé's chest and all three of them laughed.

"I just remembered my dad telling me to go for it before I lost you, you know," Corey said, still looking down but smiling proudly. "So, I did."

“I’m proud of you, son,” Corey said, hugging them both again. “I’ll be right back, I just have to make a call.”

He went into his office and locked the door behind him, pulling out his phone. He needed to take his own advice, but there was something he needed to do first.

“Darren?” Sheila sounded surprised to hear from him.

"What did I do wrong?" he asked without beating around the bush. "At least, tell me that."

"You didn't do anything wrong, Darren," she said in that sweet and reassuring voice. She didn’t even ask what he was talking about. God, once upon a time that voice had been his rock when he was down. When had he stopped going to her when he needed support?

"At least, nothing that we aren't both guilty of," she continued. "I think we just stopped caring. Stopped checking in. We let ourselves get too comfortable in the knowledge that we cared about each other and stopped doing things that actually showed that we cared."

“But how do I stop that from happening again?” he asked.

“You’ve met someone?” she asked, interested.

“I did, but I messed it up,” he said. “I don’t want the same thing that happened with us to happen again.”

“You can’t live in fear of relationships forever, Darren,” she said sounding disapproving. “I know it seems like you failed in our marriage, but you didn’t. We both made mistakes and took each other for granted. So, if you don’t want that to happen you just have to make that conscious effort. It’s not rocket science, you know?”

They shared a laugh at that and Darren knew what he had to do.

“Thank you, Sheila,” he said. “I’m sorry it didn’t work out between you and your guy, but I hope you know you’re an amazing woman. Anyone would be lucky to be with you."

"Thanks, Darren. Now, go and get that girl."

Laughing at the irony of his wife saying that to him, Darren hung up and stepped out of his office. With a goodbye to Corey and some other staff members, he sped off to Amelia's house.

She lived in an apartment complex that was only about 20 minutes from the office. He knocked on her door, feeling his nerves build up but pushing them down with determination.

"Darren?"

Amelia was dressed down for the evening, wearing a pair of shorts and a tank top. Her long dark curls were pulled up in a messy bun and her green eyes sparked behind a pair of reading glasses.

"What are you doing here?"

"You were right," he said.

"Right?"

"That night at my office." He didn't have to specify what night he meant. Though they had spent many nights together in that office, getting to know each other and building a strong foundation, they both knew the night he was referring to. "You were right. There is something between us. Of course, there is. I was scared, and I hurt you and I'm so sorry, Amelia."

She looked stunned at his confession.

"I think you should come in," she said finally. She shut the door behind him and turned around to face him.

"Say something," he pleaded.

"What were you scared of?" she asked.

"Of messing things up the way I did with Sheila," he confessed.

"What happened with Sheila wasn't just your fault."

"I know that now." He took a step closer. "And if you'll have me, I'm willing to try with you. God, I really want to try with you,

Amelia. I'm crazy about you. Your vibrancy and passion inspire me."

She remained silent for a few moments and Darren wondered if she was going to kick him to the curb. But then a small smile began to grow on her face and she threw herself into his arms.

He wrapped her in a tight hug. "Is that a yes?" he asked hopefully.

"It's a 'kiss me right now'!" she replied, giggling.

They kissed then, a kiss filled with love and hope for a bright future. Their arms wrapped around each other tight as their lips softly explored each other.

"I'm crazy about you too," she whispered against his lips. "And I think you should take me to the bedroom."

He walked them into her bedroom and lay her down on the bed.

She sat back up instantly, scrambling out of her clothes, causing him to laugh as he did the same.

"Someone is eager," he teased.

"I've been wanting to do this for months."

When she got her shirt and shorts off, Darren stopped her and reached down.

"Let me."

He slowly took off her remaining garments and then stripped off the last of his clothes and leaned over her, covering her with kisses as they became truly one with each other.

Afterward, they lay cuddled in the bed. Amelia had already drifted off and Darren looked down at her. He would not mess this up. Not this time.

Caution

You pick your sizzle factor for MA audience is beyond this page. Stop here if you've read enough.

Don't forget to leave a review for us if you'd like us to continue this series.

Showdown

Amelia was a fool.

She had been an idiot to think that she stood a chance with Darren but became a certified fool when she had walked out of his office that night and lingered at the door, waiting for him to come after her. He never had and now, two months later, they had lost that easy connection that had built so beautifully between them.

Bella had eventually reached out to her, and both she and Darren had been present as the young girl shared her story. The governor had done more than just touch her inappropriately at the office but had assaulted her countless times, forcing kisses and unwanted touches on her whenever he gave her a trip home after work.

He kept her silent with the threat of ruining her name if she spoke up, but Darren assured her that he wouldn't let that happen. After they had heard Bella's testimony, Amelia wanted nothing more than to talk to Darren, share her feelings and fears and listen to his thoughts on the matter. Instead, they had shared a charged look but ultimately gone their separate ways.

And that was why Amelia considered herself a fool. Because after everything she still believed that he wanted her, that he had feelings. She didn't know why he was denying them, and she wasn't fully convinced that she wasn't being completely delusional.

Nevertheless, they continued to work together until the trail day eventually approached.

"Are you nervous?" she asked him as they sat in the courtroom waiting for the judge to arrive.

“I should be asking you that,” he responded.

“I'm never nervous when you're with me.” Her reply was more honest than she wanted it to be, but it was the truth. Darren made her feel brave.

Her words seemed to shock him but before he could respond, the judge arrived, and the trial began.

It was a harsh back and forth between the two sides, but Amelia was proud to see Darren hold his ground the whole time. He made a passionate opening statement, citing Amelia's years of work and the governor's charming façade. As the trial went on, the opposition brought forth witnesses to attest to the governor's good name, and Amelia herself had to testify.

But it was Bella's testimony that brought the case home. The whole court was silent as the young girl recounted her experience with the governor. Bella wasn't the crying girl Amelia had held in her home on the stand. Instead, she was the strong-willed and determined young woman Amelia had witnessed countless times in the office. She didn't allow her voice to waver as she talked about the way the governor forced kisses on her and grabbed her in his car then dropped her off at her home with a threat to remain silent.

With Bella's testimony over and the jury gone off to deliberate, Amelia knew that the case was theirs.

"We have a celebratory party," Darren informed her. "After every big case, we win. It's on Friday at the office if you want to come."

They were standing outside the courthouse after the judge had declared the governor guilty, and while Amelia felt pride and satisfaction in their hard work, the feeling was bittersweet. With the case over, she truly had to say goodbye to Darren, and she wasn't sure if she was ready for that.

"I'll think about it," she said with a shrug, knowing that she probably wouldn't show up. It was better to end things now than to drag it out.

"Okay," he said.

She waited still, foolishly, hoping he would say something, but he just walked away.

*

Darren knew something was wrong when he didn't even want to celebrate. It was another win for the firm and a personal win for him, but he felt dejected as he stood amidst his partying staff.

"You okay, dad?" Corey asked.

"Yes, son, I'm fine."

"You sure?" he pressed. "You don't look like someone who just won a sexual assault case against a governor."

Darren gave a small laugh at his son's words.

"I guess I'm just tired."

Corey hummed noncommittally. "Is Amelia going to come?"

That was the question, wasn't it?

"I don't know," Darren replied honestly.

"Hey, baby." Corey's girlfriend, Christine wrapped her arm around him from behind and placed a kiss on his cheek.

“Hey, Darren, congratulations again on the win,” she said.

“Thank you, Christy.”

“Did Corey share the big news yet?” she asked.

"Big news?" Darren looked at his son confused.

“Oh, babe, I don’t know if this is the right time,” he trailed off as Darren’s gaze landed on the ring on Christine’s finger.

“You did it!” he exclaimed, pulling the two of them in for a hug. “I’m so happy for you both!”

“Thanks, dad,” Corey said bashfully.

"It took him long enough!" Christine playfully slapped her fiancé's chest and all three of them laughed.

"I just remembered my dad telling me to go for it before I lost you, you know," Corey said, still looking down but smiling proudly. "So, I did."

"I'm proud of you, son," Corey said, hugging them both again. "I'll be right back, I just have to make a call."

He went into his office and locked the door behind him, pulling out his phone. He needed to take his own advice, but there was something he needed to do first.

"Darren?" Sheila sounded surprised to hear from him.

"What did I do wrong?" he asked without beating around the bush. "At least, tell me that."

"You didn't do anything wrong, Darren," she said in that sweet and reassuring voice. She didn't even ask what he was talking about. God, once upon a time that voice had been his rock whenever he was down. When had he stopped going to her when he needed support?

"At least, nothing that we aren't both guilty of," she continued. "I think we just stopped caring. Stopped checking in. We let ourselves get too comfortable in the knowledge that we cared about each other and stopped doing things that actually showed that we cared."

"But how do I stop that from happening again?" he asked.

"You've met someone?" she asked, interested.

"I did, but I messed it up," he said. "I don't want the same thing that happened with us to happen again."

"You can't live in fear of relationships forever, Darren," she said sounding disapproving. "I know it seems like you failed in our marriage, but you didn't. We both made mistakes and took each other for granted. So, if you don't want that to happen you just have to make that conscious effort. It's not rocket science, you know?"

They shared a laugh at that, and Darren knew what he had to do.

"Thank you, Sheila," he said. "I'm sorry it didn't work out between you and your guy, but I hope you know you're an amazing woman. Anyone would be lucky to be with you."

"Thanks, Darren. Now, go and get that girl."

Laughing at the irony of his wife saying that to him, Darren hung up and stepped out of his office. With a goodbye to Corey and some other staff members, he sped off to Amelia's house.

She lived in an apartment complex that was only about 20 minutes from the office. He knocked on her door, feeling his nerves build up but pushing them down with determination.

"Darren?"

Amelia was dressed down for the evening, wearing a pair of shorts and a tank top. Her long dark curls were pulled up in a messy bun and her green eyes sparked behind a pair of reading glasses.

"What are you doing here?"

"You were right," he said.

"Right?"

"That night at my office." He didn't have to specify what night he meant. Though they had spent many nights together in that office, getting to know each other and building a strong foundation, they both knew the night he was referring to. "You were right. There is something between us. Of course, there is. I was scared, and I hurt you and I'm so sorry, Amelia."

She looked stunned at his confession.

"I think you should come in," she said finally. She shut the door behind him and turned around to face him.

"Say something," he pleaded.

"What were you scared of?" she asked.

"Of fucking things up the way I did with Sheila," he confessed.

"What happened with Sheila wasn't just your fault."

"I know that now." He took a step closer. "And if you'll have me, I'm willing to try with you. God, I really want to try with you,

Amelia. I'm crazy about you. Your vibrancy and passion inspire me."

She remained silent for a few moments and Darren wondered if she was going to kick him to the curb. But then a small smile began to grow on her face, and she threw herself into his arms.

He wrapped her in a tight hug. "Is that a yes?" he asked hopefully.

"It's a 'kiss me right now'!" she replied, giggling.

They kissed then, a kiss filled with love and hope for a bright future. Their arms wrapped around each other tight as their lips softly explored each other.

"I'm crazy about you too," she whispered against his lips. "And I think you should take me to the bedroom."

Their kisses became less chase then, as they plundered each other's mouths. Amelia moaned breathily as Darren nibbled on her lip and hoisted her up so she could wrap her legs around his waist. He walked them into her bedroom and lay her down on the bed.

She sat back up instantly, scrambling out of her clothes, causing him to laugh as he did the same.

“Someone is eager,” he teased.

“I’ve been wanting to do this for months.”

When she got her shirt and shorts off, Darren stopped her and reached down.

“Let me.”

He slowly took off her underwear, revealing her perky breast and the wetness between her legs.

“Please, Darren, don’t make me wait any longer.”

They didn't exchange any more words then. He stripped off the last of his clothes and leaned over her, covering her face, neck, and breasts with kisses. Amelia writhed beneath him, arching up when he took a nipple between his lips and teased at the sensitive bud with his teeth.

He lined himself up and, with one sharp thrust, seated his hardness in her. They made matching sounds of ecstasy as they were joined most intimately, and Amelia wrapped both her arms and legs around him.

Darren took his time with it, filling her up with slow and deep thrusts that had them both panting heavily. Their bodies were covered with sweat, and he leaned his forehead against hers. Their climaxes built slowly, and he felt her grip him tighter, both internally and externally as she rode the wave of her orgasm.

He followed soon after, squeezing his eyes shut as pleasure washed over him.

Afterward, they lay cuddled in the bed. Amelia had already drifted off and Darren looked down at her. He would not mess this up. Not this time.

Did you enjoy this book?

If so, please leave a review on Amazon!

Ready for more? Follow this and other favorites below!

https://www.ttpublishinghouse.com/legendsreborn

https://www.ttpublishinghouse.com/7wishes

https://www.ttpublishinghouse.com/mallcadet

www.ingramcontent.com/pod-product-compliance
Lightning Source LLC
LaVergne TN
LVHW050329160826
845677LV00014B/3568